I0782116

MYTHS and LEGENDS

of the

WOODLAND CREE

MYTHS and LEGENDS

of the

WOODLAND CREE

As told by Elizabeth Roberts and translated by Dr. Rose Roberts

BIG MOOSE
PUBLISHING

Images on pages 1-26, 28-35, 37-51, 53-65, 67-90 were created by Stéphanie Baribeau using Microsoft Copilot, 2024.
Book Coordinators: E. Mirasty Ph.D. (ABD), and V. Brittain Ed.D. (ABD)

Published by:
Big Moose Publishing
Box 127 Site 601 RR#6
Saskatoon, SK S7K 3J9
www.bigmoosepublishing.com

ISBN: 978-1-989840-67-2
Big Moose Publishing 03/2024

A MESSAGE FROM THE CHIEF

Grand Chief Brian Hardlotte

Preserving First Nations myths and legends is crucial for several reasons: for cultural heritage, identity, spirituality, environmental stewardship, and education. As a political leader, I know many of our elders possess a rich history that are found in myths and legends.

Our First Nations' myths and legends are integral to the cultural identity of our peoples. They hold the wisdom, beliefs, and values passed down through generations, connecting individuals to their ancestors and their cultural roots. Myths and legends provide a means for First Nations people to express their unique identity and world view. They offer a platform for storytelling, art, and oral tradition, allowing individuals to connect with their heritage and express their cultural pride.

Overall, preserving First Nations myths and legends is essential for maintaining cultural continuity, fostering community resilience, and promoting understanding and appreciation of Indigenous cultures. On behalf of the Prince Albert Grand Council, I want to thank Dr. Rose Roberts and her mother Elizabeth Roberts for collecting these stories and preserving them for the next generation.

Brian Hardlotte
Grand Chief
Prince Albert Grand Council

ABOUT the AUTHORS

Elizabeth Roberts

Elizabeth Roberts (nee McLeod) was born to James and Amelia McLeod in 1938, and raised on their trapline on La Ronge Lake. She married John Roberts and her trapline then became Hickson-Maribelli Lakes. She spent over 60 freeze ups and quite a few spring thaws in that area, other seasons were spent at Otter Lake, and at her permanent home in Stanley Mission. She had 12 children, 8 of whom are still living, numerous grandchildren and great grandchildren. Her father was a halfbreed, thus Elizabeth did not have to attend a residential school, all her education is land based within the Woodland Cree culture and language. All these stories were told in the Cree language and then translated into English by her daughter Rose.

Dr. Rose Roberts

Dr. Rose Roberts grew up immersed within the Woodland Cree culture, except during those times that she attended residential school. Thanks to her mother not knowing how to speak English, Rose never lost her language as a result of residential school. She has 2 adult children and 1 grandson. She has 3 degrees from the University of Saskatchewan; Bachelor of Science in Nursing, Masters and Doctorate in Community Health & Epidemiology. Rose has spent the majority of her career teaching in university settings and living in urban settings, but she reconnected to the land of her ancestors in 2008 when she went to the trapline for her first freeze up. She grew up hearing these stories, after the kerosene lamp had been blown out, snuggled up in bed with her siblings with the fire crackling in the stove. These stories are among the best of her childhood memories.

CHICHIPSCHIKWAN

Listen to the story in Cree

Once there was a family that lived by themselves in the bush, a man and woman who were husband and wife, and their two sons. The older boy, whose name was Wesakichak, was about 12 years old. The younger one was a baby about a year old.

Every day the man went hunting and the woman stayed home and looked after the home and the boys.

TABLE of CONTENTS

One day the man began to notice a change in his wife's behaviour. She no longer kept the home tidy and she would forget to have a meal ready for him when he got home.

"What do you do with yourself all day? I come home and the teepee is cold and there is no food prepared?" he asked her.

"My husband, I go to the bathroom, and by the time I wipe my bum it is sunset," she replied.

The man asked his son Wesakichak what his mother did while he was off hunting.

"She takes an old piece of hide and a stick, and goes into the bush. I hear her laughing, but I don't see her again until you come back home," said Wesakichak.

The next day the man goes off hunting as usual, but as soon as he gets beyond the teepee, he circles back around and waits. Soon his wife comes out of the teepee, carrying an old piece of hide. She picks up a stick as she walks and heads into the bush. The man follows his wife.

The woman approaches a stump, she wraps the hide around the stump and hits it with the stick. Snakes of all different sizes come slithering out, they surround her and she plays with them, petting them and letting them slither all over her.

The man is very angry but he sneaks away and spends the day in the bush thinking of what he is going to do. When he gets home it is getting dark, once again the teepee is cold and there is no food prepared.

When his wife finally comes in, he tells her he killed a moose and that she should go get it tomorrow and he will stay home for a change.

In the morning he helps her prepare the sled and gives her specific instructions on where to find the moose. As soon as she is out of sight, he pulls out the old hide and picking up a big stick he heads for the stump. He wraps the hide around the stump and hits it with the stick, as soon as the snakes come slithering out, he kills each one. He leaves one little one. He takes a few of them with him but hides the rest.

He makes a big pot of snake soup, leaving the heads in the pot.

He sits down Wesakichak and says, "Your mother is going to be very angry when she comes home and finds out what I have done. You and your brother may not be safe. You will have to put your brother in the tihkinakan (cradle board) and hide. If your mother gets the better of me, you must run away, for she may kill you as well."

He gave Wesakichak a small pouch, and told him there were 4 objects in there that would help him if his mother was gaining on them. "Throw one behind you and it will give you some time."

As the day got later and later, the man helped Wesakichak tie his little brother into the tihkinakan and found a big bush where they were to hide.

The woman came home with an empty sled. "I went to where you said but I couldn't find the moose," she said to her husband.

"That's alright. I'll go get it tomorrow," replied the man.

She started to grab the hide and leave the teepee again.

"Wait. Wait. Here, sit down and have some soup. You must be tired and hungry," urged the man.

The woman sat down and started eating the blood red soup. "Mmmm, this is so good.

What kind of soup is this?" she asked.

"Don't you recognize your lovers?" replied the man, stirring the pot until one of the snake heads popped to the surface.

The woman screamed, "Nooooo! You will not live this night if you have killed my men." She grabbed the old piece of hide and ran out of the teepee. She ran to the stump, wrapped the hide around it and hit it with a stick. Only one little snake came out. She flew into a terrible rage and ran back to attack her husband.

Wesakichak watched from behind the bush. He saw his mother come running back and attack his father. The man and woman fought each other, the man grabbed an axe and chopped his wife's head off. The head rolled away but the body kept fighting him.

The man and headless body kept wrestling, with neither getting the upper hand. Neither would let go of the other and they slowly started rising into the sky.

You can still see them to this day when you look up at the stars. Most people refer to the constellation as the Big Dipper but the stars that make up the handle are the man, and the stars that make up the cup are the woman.

Wesakichak looked at them for as long as he could see them, then he began to realize that he could hear his mother's voice, calling for them.

"My sons, where are you?"

Wesakichak looked around and suddenly there was his mother's head rolling out of the teepee. The head was alive and it was looking for him and his brother. Wesakichak sprang from his hiding place and started running. Behind him he could hear the head – Chichipschikwan – calling to him and telling him to stop. He dared not look back. He just kept running and running.

After a time he got tired, his brother was quite heavy and he started slowing down to a fast walk. He knew he needed a break. He dug into the pouch his father had given him and pulled out an awl. He threw it behind him and said, "let there be a long row of thorn bushes." And a tall thick walk of thorny bushes sprang up. He looked back and breathed a sigh of relief. He slowed to a walk, catching his breath.

Meanwhile, on the other side of the thorny bush Chichipschikwan would try rolling into the bushes, only to get her hair tangled and her skin scratched up. She rolled back and forth along the edge looking for a way through. Then she heard the crunching sound of a wood eating worm (motew) chewing through some wood.

"Motew, you handsome thing, come out and show yourself."

"Who is calling me?" asked the worm, poking his head out of the bark.

"It is I," replied Chichipschikwan coquettishly, "Make a tunnel for me through these thorns and I will be your wife."

"What would I do with a head, you don't even have a body," replied the worm.

"I will let you go in here," replied Chichipschikwan, referring to the small hollow behind the ear lobe (nichupskokihk).

The motew did not look impressed.

"Please motew, you are my only hope. My children are on the other side and they need me. I have to get across."

The motew took pity on Chichipschikwan and started chewing a tunnel through the thorn bushes. Chichipschikwan following close behind and as soon as she could get through, she rolled right over the worm, laughing as she rolled away and said, "As if I would every marry you!"

Wesakichak was just getting his breath back when he heard the sound of his mother coming after them, yelling, "My sons, stop. Wait for me. It is your mother."

He started running again. He ran and ran until he started to get a stitch in his side. He dug into the pouch again, this time pulling out a piece of soap. He threw it behind him and said, "Let there be a soap mountain." And a mountain made of soap sprang up behind him. He slowed down to catch his breath.

Chichipschikwan now came up to this mountain made of soap. She rolled up it but rolled back down because it was slippery. She rolled in both directions to see if she could go around it but it just kept going. Finally she stopped and said, "I had this dream once that I passed through a mountain such as this." And just like that a tunnel formed through the mountain and she rolled through.

Wesakichak had resumed running as soon as he had caught his breath. He now knew that it wouldn't be long before he would hear the sound of his mother's head catching up to them. He was tiring more quickly, because he was also carrying his brother on his back.

And it didn't seem very long when he heard, "My sons, nikosisak, wait for me." Chichipschikwan had caught up with them again.

He grabbed another object from the pouch. This time it was a piece of flint that his father had used many times to start the fire in the teepee. He threw it behind him and said, "Let there be a wall of fire."

A high wall of fire sprung up between him and the rolling head that used to be his mother. He kept on running, trying to put as much distance between him and Chichipschikwan as possible.

Meanwhile, at the other side of the wall of fire Chichipschikwan rolled into the fire and rolled back out, all her hair burnt off, including her eyebrows and eyelashes. She tried rolling through again but did not make it. Then she looked up at the wall and said, "I had this dream when I was a young girl that I passed through a wall of fire." A passageway opened up through the flames and she rolled through.

It wasn't long before Wesakichak heard the head calling for them. He was so tired. He reached into the pouch and pulled out the last object; a set of beaver teeth. He said, "Let there be a river," but he tripped just as he was going to throw it behind him and instead it went in front of them.

A wide river sprang up. He ran along the bank, trying to find a way across. A pelican was swimming by and Wesakichak said, "Nisimis (younger sibling), can you take me and my brother across the river? My mother's head is chasing us and trying to kill us."

The chuchuko swam to the bank. "Yes, I will take you across. But please don't go near my neck. It is very sore today."

Wesakichak climbed onto the chuchuko's back and it carried them across the river. He got off and looked back to see how far back Chichipschikwan was. She was not far at all, and she was a frightful sight, no hair anywhere and all scratched up.

Chichipschikwan got to the river and saw the chuchuko dropping off her sons at the other side. "Chuchuko, come here," she yelled. The pelican swam toward her. "You have to take me across," she pleaded. "Those are my sons. Their dad died and I'm all they have. I have to catch up to them so I can take care of them."

The pelican looked at her and took pity on the rolling head. "I will take you across but you must stay off my neck. It is very sore today." Chichipschikwan rolled onto the pelican's back and they started across. She was very impatient, and was rolling back and forth, back and forth. She got too close to the pelican's neck.

The pelican warned, "I told you to stay off my neck." With one flick of its body, it flipped Chichipschikwan into the river.

Chichipschikwan was only a head; it couldn't swim. Wesakichak heard it say, "I may as well become a sturgeon, my sons." And that was the end of Chichipschikwan, and where the sturgeon came from.

And the beginning of the adventures of Wesakichak...

WEMISOSO
and the
SANDPIPER

Listen to the story in Cree

Wesakichak continued on, still carrying his little brother in the tihkinakan, now that the danger of being caught by Chichipschikwan was past, he wasn't sure where to go. His little brother was crying because he was hungry. Eventually they came out onto a large lake, and a beach. Wesakichak made a swing between two trees and tried to get his brother to stop crying.

A hawk flew by and landed on a tree nearby. "What is wrong?" asked the hawk.

"I'm trying to get my little brother to stop crying," replied Wesakichak.

"Take my talons off, and use them as a rattle, they will sound like bells when they hit the sand," said the hawk.

So Wesakichak removed the hawk's talons and strung them together. He threw them into the air and when they landed on the sand they tinkled like bells. His little brother stopped crying, so he kept throwing the talons into the air.

Along came Wemisoso in his canoe, he was an older man that had magical powers. To make his canoe go where he wanted, he lay in the bottom of the canoe and hit the side with the paddle. The paddle never went into the water. So anyone looking out onto the water would only see a canoe.

Wesakichak wasn't paying attention to the water, and so when Wemisoso uttered, "Let that rattle fall into my canoe," all Wesakichak saw was that when he threw the talons into the air, they arced away and fell into a canoe that was floating by.

"Bring those back," he said.

"Come and get them," replied Wemisoso.

"Give them back. They're the only thing that stops my brother crying," said Wesakichak as he waded into the water. Wemisoso stuck his paddle out and said, "Napoothtakoskih (put both feet on) and come and get them."

Wesakichak stepped onto the paddle. Wemisoso flicked him into the canoe, and took off into deep water.

"Let me out. I can't leave my little brother. Let me out," cried Wesakichak.

Wemisoso kept his canoe going further and further away.

Wesakichak could hear his brother crying. Until suddenly the crying stopped, to be replaced by a wolf howl. Wesakichak looked up and saw a white wolf running along the beach. The wolf sang, "nistisi, nistisi, kiyam nika mahikanowin (my brother, my brother, I will become a wolf)."

Wesakichak yelled back, "Promise that you will never chase your prey into the water!" And to this day wolves do not chase their prey into the water.

And then Wesakichack curled up in the front of the canoe and cried. He had lost his whole family in one day.

By and by, he felt the canoe hit land. He didn't even look up. He heard Wemisoso get out of the canoe. Wemisoso pulled up the canoe and flipped it over. Wesakichak stayed in the front and under the canoe.

Wemisoso had 2 daughters, and as he went into their teepee, he said to the older one, "I have brought you a husband. He's hiding under the canoe."

The older girl went down to the water, looked under the canoe and a red-eyed, puffy-faced boy looked back at her. She went back up the hill, "I don't want him. He's red-eyed and ugly from crying," she told her father.

Wemisoso said to the youngest, "I guess he's yours. Take a towel and some lotion with you to clean him up." The younger sister did as she was told. She went to the canoe, lifted it up and said, "Astum, (come here)," to Wesakichak.

Wesakichak crawled out and he let her wash his face and put on some lotion to bring down the puffiness. When he was all cleaned up, they went back to the teepee. As soon as the older daughter saw Wesakichak, she tried to take him away from her younger sister.

Wemisoso said, "Now, now, there is no need to fight my daughters. You can share him." And just like that, Wesakichak had 2 women!

Wesakichak stayed there, and soon both his women were pregnant and they both had sons. As time went by, the boys grew and began to copy their father. They wanted bows and arrows, so Wesakichak made them little ones.

By this time Wemisoso had gotten what he had wanted, grandsons, so he figured it was time his son-in-law disappeared. When he saw the little bows, he said to Wesakichak, "Those are pitiful. I can take you to where the willows are straight and supple, perfect for making bows and arrows."

The next day they go in the canoe and out into the lake to a remote island. As soon as Wesakichak stepped on the land, Wemisoso pushed off the canoe and said, "There is my son-in-law, nipowakan (spirit animal)."

Wesakichak turned around and could hear the sounds of a huge creature coming toward him. A giant snake slithered out of the long grasses. Wesakichak had a hatchet with him, which he had planned to use to cut down the willows, and he used that to kill the snake.

By this time, Wemisoso was long gone, believing that the snake would kill Wesakichak. Wesakichak cut enough willows to make his sons bows and arrows, and he also cut the snake's head off. Then he turned himself into a huge seagull, and started flying home.

In the middle of the lake he saw his father-in-law, sleeping in the canoe. He swooped down and pooped right into Wemisoso's open mouth.

Wemisoso woke up spluttering and spitting. "Ah, stupid stinking seagull!" he yelled.

When Wesakichak got home, he made his sons little bows and arrows. He also tied up the snake head above Wemisoso's sleeping area.

The boys ran down to the lake when their grandfather got home, eager to show off their bows and arrows. "Nosisimak (My grandchildren), who made you those bows and arrows?" he asked.

"Our father," they replied.

"Oh, my poor grandsons, your father is gone. He got eaten by a giant snake."

"No, he didn't," they answered.

Wemisoso went up the hill and into the teepee. He saw Wesakichak sitting there, and in his shame, he put his head down and went to his sleeping area. Something dripped on him, when he looked up he saw his powakan's head dangling there. He threw himself face down and cried "Nipowakan, nipowakan."

After a few minutes, Wesakichak had had enough. "Take that head down and throw it out. I'm tired of hearing your father cry," he told his wives.

A few days later, Wemisoso heard the boys saying they wanted feathers for their arrows, so he said, "Son-in-law, I know where you can get beautiful feathers for my grandson's arrows. Come. I will take you there."

"Are you going to try and get me killed?" asked Wesakichak.

Wemisoso shook his head no. So off they went in the canoe.

Again, they went far out onto the lake to a remote island. Again, as Wesakichak stepped out of the canoe, Wemisoso says, "There you go nipowakan. I am never satisfied with my choice of son-in-law."

Wesakichak heard the loud rustle of wings and, as he turned around, a giant eagle was swooping down toward him, talons outstretched. He swung at the belly of the eagle with his hatchet before the talons could get him, and killed it. He cut the eagle's head off and harvested some feathers, then turned himself into a seagull and flew home.

Once again he came upon his father-in-law taking a nap in his canoe in the middle of the lake. Once again, he swooped down and pooped in his mouth, and kept on flying home.

Wemisoso was rudely awoken again by a stupid stinking seagull.

Wesakichak made fletching for his son's arrows and tied up the eagle head above his father-in-law's sleeping area.

When Wemisoso got home, the boys ran down to show off the feathers in their arrows.

"Nosisimak, where did those feathers in your arrows come from?" Wemisoso asked.

"Our father," they replied.

"My poor grandsons, your father is gone. He was killed by a giant eagle."

"No, he didn't," they answered.

As Wemisoso entered the teepee, there sat Wesakichak. His head down in shame, Wemisoso went to his sleeping area and sat down. Something dripped on him and when he looked up he saw his powakan's head swinging above him. He threw himself face down and cried, "Nipowakan, misi-mikisew, you have killed nipowakan."

After a few minutes, Wesakichak said to his wives, "Take that head down and throw it out. I'm tired of hearing your father cry."

After a few days had passed, Wemisoso was even more intent on getting rid of his son-in-law.

He said, "Son-in-law, my grandsons should have strong sinew for their bows and to tie up the feathers on their arrows. I know where you can get some."

Wesakichak said to his father-in-law, "You're not trying to get me killed again are you?"

Wemisoso shook his head no and off they went in his canoe; far out onto the lake to a remote island. When Wesakichak stepped on the shore, Wemisoso pushed off and said, "There he is nipowakan."

A huge moose came crashing through the bushes, swinging his antlers back and forth. Wesakichak didn't waste any time killing it. He cut the head off, and took the long tendons (astisiyah) from the back of the moose that is made into sinew. He turned himself into a huge seagull again and flew back home, pooping in Wemisoso's mouth as he lay snoring in his canoe.

Wesakichak got home and carried the big moose head up the hill, it was very heavy. He tied it above his father-in-law's sleeping area. And then he set about fastening the feathers to the arrows using the sinew he had collected.

Wemisoso didn't get back until late in the day. His grandsons ran down to show him their arrows.

"Eee, nosimisak, who put the feathers on your arrows?"

"Our father," they replied.

Muttering to himself he said, "How is that possible?" And then to the boys, "That's not possible. I fed your father to my powakan misi-mooswah."

He entered the teepee, and seeing Wesakichak sitting there with his daughters, he hung his head in shame and went to his sleeping area. As he sat down he bumped his head on something. When he looked up, it was the head of his powakan. He threw himself on his blankets wailing, "Nipowakan misi-mooswah. Nipowakan. You have been killed." He was also thinking, *"How does he do this? How does he keep defeating nipowakanak?"*

After a few minutes Wesakichak said to his wives, "Throw that head out. I'm tired of listening to your father's cry." It took both of the women to lift it and take it outside.

He said to his wives, "I'm going to leave. Your father keeps on trying to kill me. I'm going to go look for my brother."

The next morning he packed up a few things and got ready to go. Wemisoso asked, "Where are you going son-in-law?"

One of his daughters replied, "He's leaving. He says you keep trying to kill him."

"I do not. I just take him to where he can get the best materials for my grandsons," Wemisoso replied indignantly.

"He's leaving just the same," replied his daughter. "He wants to go look for his brother."

"I'll walk with you part way, and show you the way we had come back then," Wemisoso said to Wesakichak. They started walking, keeping close to the shoreline. They came to small bay and Wesakichak says, "Let's split up here. You go that way and I'll go this way. Whatever type of feather we find, we will change ourselves to that bird and fly across the bay."

So they split up.

Wesakichak whispered to himself, "I wish to find the feather of a cheecheeskisees (sandpiper), and that Wemisoso finds the feather of a weeskachans (gray jay)." By now Wesakichak was coming into his own magical powers. And sure enough, he finds a feather of a cheecheeskisees.

"Did you find a feather?" he yells at Wemisoso.

"Yes, I found the feather of a weeskachans," replied Wemisoso.

"I'll go first," volunteered Wesakichak. He turned himself into a cheecheeskisees and flew across the bay. When he was about halfway across, Wemisoso clapped his hands loudly and sang out, "He's not going to make it. He's not going to make it."

The sounds startled Wesakichak, but sandpipers are very adept flyers, and they are used to water. Although he almost fell into the water, he skimmed along it and landed on a rock close to shore.

"Your turn," he said to Wemisoso.

"Don't try and scare me now," Wemisoso said.

"I won't," replied Wesakichak.

Wemisoso turned himself into a weeskachans and lifted off. Wesakichak waited until he was in the middle of the bay and he clapped and yelled, "He's not going to make it. He's not going to make it."

The sounds startled Wemisoso and he fell into the water. Weeskachans are good flyers, but not necessarily around the water. When he hit the water, he turned back into a man. Since he couldn't swim, he started sinking.

Wesakichak watched as his father-in-law sank into the water. Pretty soon the only thing sticking out was Wemisoso's pointer finger so Wesakichak shot it with his bow and arrow until it was out of sight. And that was the end of Wemisoso.

WESAKICHAK and the SEALS

Listen to the story in Cree

Wesakichak continued on his search for his brother, who had turned into a wolf when he was a baby. He came upon wolf tracks so he started following them. He knew these tracks were those of his brother. He followed the tracks to a beach and saw that they led into the water.

"Oh nisimis, I told you not to chase your prey into the water."

As he stood on the beach looking out into the water, he saw a couple of athkikwak (seals) playing with something white in the water. As he continued to watch, he saw that it was a white wolf pelt. The athkikwak came ashore and they were followed by others.

A kingfisher landed on a branch near him. "What are they doing?" Wesakichak asked. He could talk to all the animals now.

"They come ashore in the evening and play with the wolf pelt," answered the kingfisher.

"That's my brother. They killed my brother," thought Wesakichak. He found a place to sit and watch without being seen by the seals.

More and more landed on the beach. They threw the wolf pelt at each other, played tug of war with it. Some just lay on the beach watching.

Wesakichak was getting angrier and angrier. They had killed his brother. He noticed that one of the seals was bigger than the rest and was merely watching the others playing. He figured this was the leader.

Wesakichak dug in his pouch and pulled out a spike made from the pickerel's top fin. He threw the spike at the leader and got it lodged deep in its neck.

All the seals rushed back into the water.

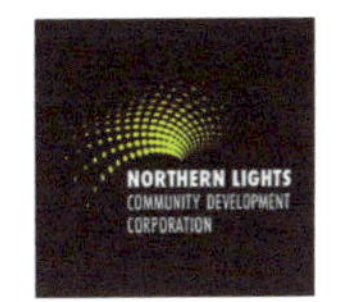 

Wesakichak stayed nearby. The next day, two seals came out of the water, and as they came closer to him they said, "We are looking for medicine for our okimow (leader). He got attacked yesterday and if he sinks and dies, so too will the earth sink."

"Let me go with you," offered Wesakichak, "I'm a medicine man." So the two seals took him to their camp.

"Which one is your okimow in?" he asked.

"In that big teepee on the other side," they replied.

Wesakichak headed in that direction. When he got to the teepee he said, "I'm a medicine man. I heard your okimow is sick and I'm here to help."

He was shown into the teepee. Inside it was dark and damp, the okimow seal lay humped over, whimpering in pain. Wesakichak said, "I need privacy. I can't do my healing with anyone watching me."

All the seals left the teepee and closed the doorway.

Wesakichak went closer to the okimow seal and taking a good grip of the spike, he pushed it in with as much strength as he had, and killed the seal.

The water was already rushing into the teepee as Wesakichak ran out. The earth was beginning to flood. He ran away as fast as he could. He got to high ground and quickly built a huge raft. He invited as many animals as he could fit on there. And, they watched as the earth disappeared under water.

On the fourth day, Wesakichak decided it was time to rebuild the earth. He asked for volunteers of the water animals to go look for some earth.

Nigik (otter) volunteered to go look. Wesakichak tied a rope to its tail and down went Nigik. Soon the rope stopped moving so Wesakichak pulled it up. Nigik had drowned.

Wesakichak blew on him and brought Nigik back to life. "I'm sorry Nistisi (older brother)," said Nigik, "I couldn't find any earth."

Amisk (beaver) volunteered next. Wesakichak tied a rope to its tail and down went Amisk.

He was gone longer than Nigik, but again the rope stopped moving. Wesakichak pulled Amisk back up. Amisk had drowned. Wesakichak blew on him and brought Amisk back to life.

When Amisk had regained his senses, he said, "I'm sorry Nistisi, I couldn't find any earth either."

Wachuskoos (muskrat) came forward. "I will try Nistisi," she said.

Wesakichak tied the rope on her tail and she went into the water. She was gone for a long time, much longer than Nigik and Amisk. But again the rope stopped moving, and Wesakichak pulled Wachuskoos back up. She had drowned, but clenched in her tiny paws was some mud.

Wesakichak blew on her and brought her back to life.

"You did it nisimis!" said Wesakichak.

He took the small bits of mud and formed a tiny ball. Then he blew on it and it got bigger.

He sang as he continued to roll the ball and blow on it. It got bigger and bigger. Soon it was too big to hold. Then, it was too big to sit on the raft. Still Wesakichak sang and blew on it.

The ball grew bigger and bigger. Soon there were trees and grass and rocks. Mountains formed. Lakes, rivers and oceans. Finally, Wesakichak stopped singing and blowing.

"I think the earth is big enough now," he said. "Kakakoo (raven) go see if I have made it big enough."

Kakakoo flies off, it takes him one day and one night before he returns.

"Is it big enough nisimis?" asked Wesakichak.

Kakakoo nods his head.

Wesakichak steps closer to it, "Why do you smell like poop?"

Kakakoo swallows what he was eating.

"Kakakoo, from this day forth you will be a scavenger, eating poop and whatever else you can find!" declared Wesakichak.

"Nisimis Ahasoo (crow), go and see if the earth is big enough?"

So Ahasoo flies off. She is gone for 2 days and 2 nights. When she returns, her beak is full of berries. She drops them at Wesakichak's feet. "Nistisi, the earth is beautiful. There is plenty of food for everyone."

The animals left the raft and scattered in all directions. Wesakichak stepped on the new earth and started walking.

WESAKICHAK
and the
GROUSE

Listen to the story in Cree

Wesakichak was walking along and he stumbled onto a nest of baby grouse. He asked them, "Where is your mother?"

"She went looking for berries," they said.

"When will she be back?" asked Wesakichak.

"We don't know Nistisi, she never told us," replied the oldest of the baby grouse.

"Oh, I'm sooo hungry, but you guys are so puny. There's no way I would be full," remarked Wesakichak. So he took a big poop and wiped his bum with the necks of every one of those baby grouse. Then, he continued on his way.

When the mother grouse came back she kept smelling something stinky. She asked her children, "Why do you stink?"

The oldest one spoke up. "Wesakichak was here and he said we were too puny to eat so he had a poop and used our necks to wipe himself."

This angered the mother grouse. "I'll get him for this," she told herself, and flew off to gather as many grouse as she could find.

"Wesakichak used my babies' necks to wipe his bum with," she told them. "I'm going to make him pay. Will you help me?" They all agreed. Wesakichak often followed the same path in his travels and this was a well trodden one. The mother grouse said, "There is a creek up ahead that he has to cross. We will hide in the grass, and when he jumps over the creek we will all fly up and make him fall in."

So they all flew ahead to the creek that Wesakichak would have to cross, and hid in the tall grass on both sides, and waited.

Eventually Wesakichak arrived at the creek. "Here he comes," the grouse whispered amongst each other.

"There's my crossing. Time for me to jump across again," Wesakichak said to himself. He talked to himself all the time, since he didn't come across other humans very often.

The creek was fairly wide, but narrow enough that he could leap across it. He took off running. Right at the exact moment he was in the middle, all of the grouse flew up. Now if you have even heard one grouse take flight, you know how noisy they can be. Startled, Wesakichak tried to turn back around. Down he fell into the creek with a big splash.

He came up sputtering and mumbling, "Stupid noisy birds that startled me!" Wesakichak climbed onto the bank. He kept his pipe and pouch of tobacco tied to his waist. And when he checked himself over, his tobacco pouch was missing.

"I must have dropped it in the creek," he said and waded back in. His tobacco pouch lay at the bottom of the creek. He stuck his hand in to grab his pouch but all he kept grabbing was handfuls of mud.

"What is going on here," he mused. He looked up and there was his tobacco pouch snagged on a willow branch overhanging the creek.

All that time he had been trying to grab a reflection. He laughed at himself for his foolishness, snagged his pouch from the branch, and said, "Oh thank goodness, my tobacco didn't get wet."

He sat down and began filling up his pipe. Once he had a smoke and dried off a bit, he started walking again.

WESAKICHAK
and the
STONEWORTS

58

Listen to the story in Cree

Wesakichak was very hungry as he walked along. He had not had much luck with hunting the past couple of days.

He sat down to have a smoke by some cliffs. As he was filling his pipe he heard mumbling. He looked around but didn't see any animals or humans. He could still hear the muted mumbling.

"Where is that talking coming from?" he wondered.

He didn't see anything. He did notice that the cliff was covered with black stoneworts. He leaned his head closer, but now he didn't hear anything.

"Was that you that was talking?" he asked.

One of the stoneworts replied mumbling, "Yes, that was us."

"Can you be eaten?" he asked.

"Yes, but we make one fart really bad," the stonewort replied.

"I'm sooo hungry," said Wesakichak, as he started pulling off the stoneworts and eating them. They were very crunchy. Once he felt full, he resumed walking.

Soon he saw a grouse. He notched an arrow in his bow and took aim. Just when we was ready to let go of the arrow, he let out a loud fart. The noise spooked the grouse and it flew away. He didn't kill it.

He kept on walking.

Next he saw a rabbit sitting under a fir tree. *"Ah, finally I'm going to eat,"* he thought to himself as he snuck in closer. Just as he was ready to let go of his arrow, he let out a series of loud farts.

"Argh, this loud stinky koochak (bum) of mine is scaring away all the game. Just you wait koochak, you are going to say boo-boo," he said.

He went in search of a rock. He found a nice sharp one sticking out of the earth. He built a big fire around it and when the fire died down, the rock was red hot. Wesakichak pushed aside his breech cloth and sat on the rock. His farts came out really fast now.

Suddenly he came to. He was crawling around on the ground. The last thing he remembered was sitting on the rock. He realized that he must have fallen off the rock, because it was so hot. He sat himself back on the rock. It was still hot, and he didn't get off until all his farts were gone. Then, he got up and went on his way again.

A few days later, he was passing nearby. All Wesakichak did was walk around. He didn't have a home.

When night fell he slept on the ground, and sometimes he followed the same trail he had been on before. He noticed a dark brown thing lying on the ground. It looked like a piece of kathkewak (dried moose meat). He picked it up, yelled out, "Neekah (mother), you dropped your kathkewak!"

Of course nobody answered him. "What am I saying? No one is going to answer me. I may as well eat it because I am so hungry," he said to himself.

He took a bite and as he walked and chewed, a little bird landed on a nearby branch and sang, "Wesakichak omikih michew (Wesakichak is eating his scab)."

"You're lying," he said to the little bird. "This is a piece of kathkewak my mother dropped."

65

The little bird flew off and landed a little further ahead and sang again, "Wesakichak omikih michew."

Wesakichak paused, wondering if the little bird was telling the truth. He reached behind him, under his breech cloth, and all he felt was raw skin. He had sat on a red hot rock so of course he had burned himself.

"Pithesees (bird) you are telling the truth. This is my scab," he said. He threw his scab onto a nearby birch and it stuck there. "From this day on you will be known as pusakan (chaga)," Wesakichak declared.

And that pusakan is said to be very good medicine. That is Wesakichak's scab.

WESAKICHAK and the CARIBOU

Listen to the story in Cree

Wesakichak was walking along, hungry as usual, when he came upon a single caribou.

"Nisimis, are you here by yourself?" he asked.

"Yes Nistisi, there are lots of cranberries around here and I'm eating them," replied the caribou.

"I'll stay here with you then, and help you gather the cranberries."

So Wesakichak would gather the cranberries and bring them to the caribou. He was being helpful but really he was just trying to fatten up the caribou. So he kept feeding it and feeding it.

Takwakin (fall) came along and the caribou was now so fat that his tail was barely visible.

Wesakichak went in search of a sheer cliff. He was getting ready to kill the caribou. He found a nice flat area that ended in a high, sharp drop to the ground. He saw rocks littered the bottom. The perfect place.

"Now to get nisimis over here," he said to himself as he walked back to where the caribou was still eating.

"Nisimis, let's go for a walk," he said. "We have been in the same place for a long time.

So off they went. As they walked, Wesakichak picked up a handful of cranberries. As they got closer to the cliff he pretended to squeeze them into his eyes and he said, "Nisimis, try this. It makes your eyesight clearer."

The caribou stood still so Wesakichak could squeeze some cranberry juice into his eyes. Of course, now the caribou couldn't see very well; his eyes were burning from the juice.

"Let's race Nisimis," urged Wesakichak as they got to the flat area. They took off running and as they approached the drop off, Wesakichak stopped... but the caribou kept on going because he couldn't see very well. He fell over.

Wesakichak waited a few minutes, then he looked over the edge. The caribou lay dead at the bottom of the cliff. Wesakichak was happy. He went down and butchered the caribou.

He made a smoke house and smoked the meat. He collected fat in the bladder of the caribou, but the fat wouldn't harden fast enough.

He went down to the water, tied the bladder closed and put it in the water, trying to cool it off quicker. He saw a wachuskoos (muskrat) swimming by. "Astum (come here) nisimis," he said. The wachuskoos came swimming over.

"Cool off this fat for me," said Wesakichak.

"Okay," replied wachuskoos, "tie it to may tail."

Wesakichak tied the rope to wachuskoos' tail. "Don't go far, just near here."

"Okay," Wachuskoos said as it swam off but the rope wasn't long enough and his sharp little rear claws hit the bladder and popped it open. Caribou fat ran out onto the water.

Wesakichak ran into the water crying, "Nipimemees (my fat), nipimemees." He tried to scoop it back up but with the bladder broken he had no place to put it.

He yelled, "Pitheeseesak (birds) astum." As each bird arrived, he scooped some fat and smeared it on their breast bone.

And that is why to this day birds always have fat on their breast bone, because Wesakichak smeared them with caribou fat.

MISTAHI-MUSKOSKWEW (BIG BEAR WOMAN)

Listen to the story in Cree

There was this little girl that had a temper and when she got mad she would stomp off into the woods. Her mother warned her that she could meet up with a bear, but she didn't listen. One day she got angry and went off by herself into the woods. Suddenly a paw covered her mouth, grabbed her and ran off with her.

It was a big bear, he took her back to his den and kept her there. She lived with him and learned how to talk to the bear. She grew older and one day she gave birth to 2 boys. The boys were human even though their father was the bear.

A few months later the bear said to her, "We are going to be found soon. Men will come. Take my nails, put them on when you are angry."

So the woman took off his nails, tied them up in a piece of cloth and put them away.

It wasn't long before men arrived, cutting through the den walls. The woman grabbed her sons and went to the farthest corner of the den. The bear stuck his head out from the hole and he was killed right away.

One of the babies whimpered and the men heard him. They made the hole in the den bigger and they saw the woman holding 2 babies. "Oh we are so sorry. We didn't know," said the men. "Why didn't you yell or something?"

"It's okay," said the woman. "It's time I lived with humans again." So she went back with the men and lived in the village.

As the boys grew older she told them to never pretend to be bears. But that was one of the favourite games among the other children. Two children would hide behind the trees on both

sides of a path and then the other children ran by, they would jump out pretending to be bears and grab them.

One evening the other children said to Mistahi-maskoskwew's sons, "You be the bears this time. You never take your turn."

"Our mother told us we were never to pretend to be bears," said one of them.

"No, it's your turn," the others insisted.

So the two boys hid behind the trees and waited for the other children to run by. When the children ran by, they were chased by 2 big bears. The boys had turned into bears. Their mother had told them not to pretend to be bears.

As soon as the men in the village heard the children screaming, they came running out. Seeing the two bears chasing their children, they brought out their weapons and killed the two bears.

Mistahi-maskoskwew heard the screaming and she too ran out to see what was going on. She watched as one of the big bears landed close to her teepee, and the other one lay a distance away. Her two sons were dead.

She flew into a rage. She went back into her teepee, and found her husband's nails. She put them on her hands and she ran back outside, and attacked everyone. She would slap them on the back and then pull down with her nails, ripping them wide open. She killed everyone in the village, except one young girl that she had taken a liking to.

The young girl she called awahkan (slave) and made her do all the work. Awahkan went to get the water, cooked the food, got the wood, cleaned the teepee, kept the fire going. At night when they went to bed, after Awahkan had covered up. Mistahi-maskoskwew would then lay large pieces of wood all along the edge of Awahkan's blanket covers. In the morning Mistahi-maskoskwew would say "kootawih (make the fire) Awahkan." And this is the way the two of them lived for quite a while.

One day when Awahkan was out gathering wood, she came upon a man with only one leg. It was her older brother. He had left the village to go live with a female wolf when Awahkan was just a baby so she did not remember him. He was out checking beaver lodges, hunting for beaver.

"I am your brother," he said to her.

She told him what had happened at the village and that she was the only one that didn't get killed, but that Mistahi-maskoskwew treated her like a slave. "She even puts logs around my blankets when I go to sleep so I won't try to escape."

He gave her a grouse that he had killed.

"I can't take this back with me. Mistahi-maskoskwew will know that you gave it to me," she said.

"Tell her you killed it by throwing rocks at it," he told his sister, "and you have to escape tonight. Come back this way. There's a lake nearby and I will be hunting beaver there." So Awahkan took the grouse back with her.

"Where did you get that from?" asked Mistahi-maskoskwew.

"I threw rocks at it and killed it," Awahkan replied.

"You're lying. Your brother gave them to you!"

"You killed everyone. I don't have a brother," answered Awahkan.

"You have a brother. He's only got one leg," Mistahi-maskoskwew replied. "You can cook that for yourself since your brother gave it to you," she added.

That evening a big wind started blowing. Awahkan was happy because she knew when there was a big wind that Mistahi-maskoskwew slept really hard. So that night when Mistahi-maskoskwew was going to put the wood around her, Awahkan said, "Can you not put that wood around me? It makes it really hard for me to get up in the morning to make the fire."

Mistahi-maskoskwew listened to her and did not put the wood to weigh down her blankets. Awahkan waited until the wee hours of the morning, when most of us are sleeping deeply, to squirm out of her blankets. She was as quiet as could be, the sound of the wind blowing through the trees helped to mask any sounds she made. She picked up her moccasins and tiptoed out of the teepee. Only when she was quite a distance away did she put her moccasins on and start running. There was snow on the ground so she had no trouble finding her path and the direction her brother had told her to go.

It was full morning by the time she got to the lake, and there was her brother, breaking open a beaver lodge just as he said he would be.

"Keep running," he said to her, "just follow my trail. When you get to the den your sister-in- law will growl at you. Just say, 'It's me grandmother. It's me,' and she won't harm you."

Awahkan kept on running until her brother's trail ended at a den. She heard a growl coming from within. Listening to what her brother had told her she said, "It's me grandmother. It's me." The growling stopped and she crawled inside. Once inside she saw a huge female wolf laying against one of the den walls, nursing wolf pups.

Meanwhile Mistahi-maskoskwew had woken up and yelled, "Kootawih Awahkan." But there was no noise. The usual clatter of wood being removed from her blankets as she got up was missing. She looked over. The sleeping place was empty. "I knew it. I knew her brother had given her that grouse." She quickly made herself breakfast and then started chasing after Awahkan.

Mistahi-maskoskwew came upon Awahkan's brother. "Where is she? Where is Awahkan?" she asked angrily.

"I don't know. You are the one that lives with her," he replied.

"I'm going to kill her when I catch her," threatened Mistahi-maskoskwew, running past him and following the trail. She got to the den and heard the female wolf growl but paid it no heed.

Awahkan was sitting in the den, as far back from the opening as possible, terrified when she heard the footsteps approaching in the snow. "She's going to kill me nokom," she said to the wolf.

The wolf jumped out of the den. There was a brief scuffle and then it was all silent. The female wolf came back in, licking her muzzle. She had killed Mistahi-maskoskwew.

So Awahkan lived with her brother and his partner.

She had noticed that there was a bag hanging from the ceiling way in the back. Her brother had told her not to bother it. But her curiosity got the better of her one day and she took a peek; inside she found her brother's leg! She didn't know what to make of that so she didn't say anything.

As the days passed Awahkan became more and more quiet and withdrawn. Her brother noticed and asked, "what's wrong? Are you lonely?"

"Yes. When you're gone I have no one to talk to. I can't talk to her," replied Awahkan, pointing to the wolf.

"Maybe it's time you left," replied her brother. "There are people living in a village not that far away. You can go there. Take one of your nephews (wolf cubs) with you, to kill moose for you."

The wolf cubs were still little. Awahkan didn't know how a tiny wolf cub would be able to kill a moose.

Her brother told her, "When you see moose tracks, put your nephew on the tracks and turn away. No matter how much he cries do not turn back around until all is quiet."

The next morning her brother gave her directions on where she would find the village. She tucked her nephew in her shirt to keep it warm and off she went. When she came across fresh moose tracks, she took out her nephew and put him in the tracks and turned around. The little wolf pup cried pitifully as it tried to go through the snow and go from one hoof track to the next. Awahkan did not turn around until it was all quiet.

She followed the moose tracks, she saw where her nephew had had trouble making it through the snow. Suddenly they were adult wolf tracks. He must have turned big she thought to herself. She finally came out into a clearing and there lay the moose. Dead. She looked around for a big wolf but didn't see him. As she walked around the moose, she heard wolf pup whimpers coming from the back legs area of the moose. She lifted up a leg and there lay her nephew, snuggled up into the warmth of the dying moose.

Awahkan gutted the moose and took as much meat as she could carry, stuck her nephew back into her shirt and kept on walking. She reached the village and went into the first teepee she came across, inside was an old lady living on her own.

Awahkan told her what had happened to her village, and about her brother, and Mistahi- maskoskwew chasing her. When she was all done she asked, "Can I live here with you nohkom?"

The old lady said, "Yes."

So Awahkan lived with the old lady, looking after her like she had looked after Mistahi- maskoskwew.

By and by she heard that the men were not having any luck with hunting moose. Food was getting scarce as it does in the middle of winter. That evening she said to her grandmother, "I'm going hunting tomorrow, see if I have any luck."

Early the next morning Awahkan woke up and prepared for a day of hunting. She tucked her nephew in her shirt and off they went. When they came across fresh moose tracks, she put her nephew in the track and turned away. The little wolf pup cried as it struggled through the snow, trying to jump from one hoof print to the next. Soon the cries died down and when it was all quiet, Awahkan turned around and started following the trail. Once again she saw when the wolf prints turned into a full grown wolf prints.

It wasn't far when she saw the dead moose. She lifted the hind leg and there lay her nephew, snuggled into the warmth of the area. She gutted the moose and went back to the village. She told the men where she had killed the moose.

The next day the men went to retrieve the moose. They looked at the tracks, trying to figure out how one little girl could kill a moose by herself when they hadn't been able. They saw the wolf tracks. "She has a wolf helping her," they said.

When they got back to the village they went to the teepee where Awahkan lived.

"Do you have wolf with you?" they asked.

She didn't answer right away. "Why do you ask?" she replied.

"We found huge wolf prints by the moose you killed," one of them answered.

She couldn't lie. Finally she said, "Yes, but he's just little. You can't kill him. My brother gave him to me." She lifted up the fur where the little wolf pup was sleeping. They didn't harm the wolf pup. Awahkan and her nephew helped the village by killing moose from then on.